THE WEREWOLF

IN NORTHERN EUROPE, RUSSIA, AND GERMANY

By

MONTAGUE SUMMERS

This edition published by Read Books Ltd.
Copyright © 2019 Read Books Ltd.
This book is copyright and may not be
reproduced or copied in any way without
the express permission of the publisher in writing

British Library Cataloguing-in-Publication Data
A catalogue record for this book is available
from the British Library

CONTENTS

Montague Summers

Augustus Montague Summers was born in Bristol, England in 1880. He was raised as an evangelical Anglican in a wealthy family, and studied at Clifton College before reading theology at Trinity College, Oxford with the intention of becoming a Church of England priest. In 1905, he graduated with fourth-class honours, and went on to continue his religious training at the Lichfield Theological College. Summers entered his apprenticeship as a curate in the diocese of Bitton near Bristol, but rumours of an interest in Satanism and accusations of sexual misconduct with young boys led to him being cut off; a scandal which dogged him his whole life. Summers joined the growing ranks of English men of letters interested in medievalism and the occult. In 1909, he converted to Catholicism and shortly thereafter he began passing himself off as a Catholic priest, the legitimacy of which was disputed. Around this time, Summers adopted a curious attire which included a sweeping black cape and a silver-topped cane.

Summers eventually managed to make a living as a full-time writer. He was interested in the theatre of the seventeenth century, particularly that of the English Restoration, and was one of the founder members of The Phoenix, a society that performed neglected works of that era. In 1916, he was elected a fellow of the Royal Society of Literature. Summers also produced some important studies of Gothic fiction. However, his interest in the occult never waned, and in 1928, around the time he was acquainted with Aleister Crowley, he published the first English translation of Heinrich Kramer and James Sprenger's *Malleus Maleficarum* ('*The Hammer of Witches*'), a 15th century Latin text on the hunting of witches. Summers then turned to vampires, producing *The Vampire: His Kith and Kin* (1928) and

The Vampire in Europe (1929), and then to werewolves with *The Werewolf* (1933). Summers' work on the occult is known for his unusual, archaic writing style, his intimate style of narration, and his purported belief in the reality of the subjects he treats.

In his day, Summers was a renowned eccentric; *The Times* called him "*in every way a 'character'*" and "*a throwback to the Middle Ages.*" He died at his home in Richmond, Surrey.

THE WEREWOLF

THE NORTH, RUSSIA, AND GERMANY

SO immense is the wealth of tradition concerning shape-shifting contained in the ancient Sagas of the North that it becomes difficult in a strictly limited space even to indicate some of the better-known and most striking of these histories, whose legendary lore, if it is at all adequately to be examined, demands a concentrated study of no inconsiderable extension.

In Norway and Iceland those men who could assume another shape were said to be *eigi einhamir* "not of one form". The adopted shape was called by the same name as the original shape, *hamr*, and the process of transformation they called *skipta hömum* or *at hamaz*. *Hamremmi* signifies the supernatural strength thus acquired; the going about in that form was *hamför*, or *hamfarir*. A man who thus became possessed of more than human might was *hamrammr*; a man who travelled with surpassing speed therefore was *hamhleypa*.

The man borrowed the animal, with whose force he was invigorated, with whose fleetness he was endowed. He follows the instincts of the beast whose body he has made his own, but his own intelligence is neither clouded nor snuffed. The soul remains unchanged, and hence the mirror of the soul, the eye, can by no art be altered. Frigg and Freyja had their *valshamr* "falcon-mantles", attired in which they could cleave the air with the swiftness and surety of that bird. Loki, the tale went, donned one of these, and so exactly resembled a falcon that none could have discovered him save for the malicious glint of his eyes.[1]

The name for a wolf-shirt which effected the metamorphosis

7

to a wolf was *úlfahamr*,[2] and the werewolf himself was commonly known as *vargr*.[3] In modern Scandinavia the term is *varûlf*, which has been extended to include the shape-shifting to a bear, for of all the *hamrammir* none were more famous than the *berserkir* or *berserkr*,[4] the bear-sark men.[5] Twelve berserkers were the chief followers of several kings of old, as for example the Danish King Rolf Krake, King Adils, and Harald Hárfagri. In battle the berserkers were subject to fits of frenzy (*furor bersericus*)[6] termed *berserksgangr*, when they howled like wild beasts, foamed at the mouth, and bit through the iron rim of their shields. During these fits they were, according to popular belief, proof against steel and fire, and made terrible havoc in the ranks of the foe. When the fever abated they were weak and tame. In the *Icelandia Jus Ecclesiastica* the *berserksgangr* is regarded as diabolic possession, and can only be cured by religious vows.[7]

William of Auvergne, Bishop of Paris, in his *De Uniuerso*, ii, pars. iii,[8] tells of a bear in Saxony who carried off a soldier's wife, and kept her for years in a cave and knew her so that she bore him children, and when she escaped these children accompanied her in her flight. They lived for many years, and were exceedingly fierce and good soldiers. They had bear in their faces, and were called Orsini *(Ursini* from *ursus* their sire). Bishop William says that the semen ursinum so resembles the semen humanum that a child may be born of a woman.

In his *Bekerung der Norwegischen Stammes zum Christenthume*[9] Konrad Maurer relates the history of Ulfr Bjalfason, the Evening-Wolf, from the Aigla. Folk said that Ulfr was much given to shifting his shape *(hamrammr)* and he was called *kveldúlfr*, Evening-Wolf. When the werewolf fit came over him and his companions their exploits were bloody with the most ferocious savagery. Whilst the passion endured none could withstand their might, but once it had passed they were weak as water for a while.

Here it should be remarked that the Norwegian berserker were often none other than professional gangs of marauding mohocks who roamed the countryside plundering and terrorizing wherever they went. It was their wont that some bully of gigantic strength among them should challenge a landowner to "holmgang", the duello, and if the berserk conquered he would carry off his dead opponent's wife and daughters, extorting ransom, or possessing himself of the property entire. Often the titan brigand is slain by the gallant Icelandic hero.

Famous among ancient Norse stories is the legend of Sigmund the Volsung and his son Sinfjötli. It so befell that on a day in summer-tide these twain went forth through the forest, seeking spoil. And they lighted upon a certain house in the which were two men with great gold rings deeply fallen upon sleep. These were two king's sons, spell-bound skin-changers, and above them on the wall hung two wolf-shirts. Now it was the tenth day, and on that day alone were they released from the spell, and might come out of the skins. Sigmund and Sinfjötli don the shirts, but can by no means put them off, for upon them the ensorcellment had taken hold, and the weird of the king's sons must they dree, for they howled as wolves, and they understood one another as afore when they had spoken in the voice of men. So they go forth into the forest depths, adventuring, and slay many, being full weary after the slaughter. At the last they repair to the hidden house, and on the tenth day they doff the wolf-shirts, burning this gear in the fire.

Another story in the *Volsunga saga* tells how an old bitch-wolf, huge and grim, came out of the forest and night after night ate a man alive. This wolfen, it was thought, was the mother of King Siggeir, and she had shifted her shape by troll's lore and devilry.[10]

To come to a later day, Arvad August Afzelius in his *Svenska Folk-Visor Fran Forntiden* has an important note upon the "*Varulf,* eller *Man-ulf*", and also relates that a Swedish soldier from Calmar, during the last war with Russia in 1808–9, was homesick and came back in the shape of a wolf. Unluckily he was shot by a hunter just outside his native village. When the dead wolf, a huge beast, was skinned, a man's shirt was found next to the body. A woman identified it as one she had stitched for her husband before he left for the field.[11]

Albert Krantz, in his *Chronica Regnorum Aquilonarium Daniae, Suetiae, Noruagiae,* liber i, caput xxxii,[12] tells a tradition of the death of King Froto III of Denmark, before whom a witch turned her son into a calf and by glamour herself appeared as an ox. The monarch, wondering at such ensorcellment, approached too near, whereupon the ox, bellowing fiercely, charged and pierced his side with two great branching horns, of which wound the old King died presently.

The learned Joannes Tritheim, Abbot of Sponheim, in his *Annales Hirsaugienses,*[13] relates that in the year 970 there ruled over Bulgaria two brothers, Peter and Baianus, the sons of King Simeon, who had erstwhile been a monk. Now Prince Baianus was the most skilful magician of his day and wrought many a marvel which set all men agape. For by the aid of the Devil he would change himself into a wolf, or into a bird, or take whatever form of beast he list. By his evil craft and ensorcellments not unseldom did he mock and beguile the folk with these devil's delusions.

This is from the *Speculum Historiale* of Vincent of Beauvais,[14] liber xxiv, cap. 87, which concludes: "Hoc tempore [Othonis Imperatoris] Bulgaribus dominabantur filii Symeonis Petrus et Bayanus, quorum Bayanus in arte magica adeo ualebat, ut quotiens uellet Lupus, uel quaelibet fera fieri uideretur."

Olaus Magnus, in his *Historia de Gentibus Septentrionalibus,*[15] Rome, 1555, has much to say of wolves in general and devotes the last three chapters of his Eighteenth Book to werewolfery, emphasizing the hellish ferocity of the werewolf, and discussing these transformations with examples of such metamorphosis both from old days and in his own time. "In the Feast of Christs Nativity, in the night, at a certain place, that they are resolved upon among themselves, there is gathered together such a huge multitude of Wolves changed from men that dwell in divers places, which afterwards the same night doth so rage with wonderfull fiercenesse, both against mankind and other creatures, that are

10

not fierce by nature, that the Inhabitants of that Country suffer more hurt from them, than ever they do from true naturall Wolves. For as it is proved they set upon the houses of men that are in the Woods with wonderful fierceness, and labour to break down the doors, whereby they may destroy both men and other creatures that remain there. They go into Beer-Cellars, and there they drink out some Tuns of Beer or Mede . . . wherein they differ from natural and true Wolves. . . . Between *Lituania, Samogetia,* and *Curonia,* there is a certain wall left, of a Castle that was thrown down; to this at a set time some thousands of them come together, that each of them may try his nimblenesse in leaping; he that cannot leap over this wall, as commonly the fat ones cannot, are beaten with whips by their Captains. And it is constantly affirmed that amongst that multitude are the great men & chiefest Nobility of the Land."

Olaus Magnus relates how when a certain Nobleman was travelling through the woods who had many servile Country-fellows in his company that were acquainted with this witchcraft of shape-shifting, and they were not only benighted but withal sore pinched with hunger and want, when a flock of sheep was spied at a distance one of the company promised they should have a lamb to roast for supper. Presently he goes into a thicket that no man might see him, and then he changed his human shape like to a Wolf. After this he fell upon the flock with all his might, and in the form of a Wolf brought back a sheep to the Chariot. His companions being conscious how he stole it, receive it with grateful mind, and hide it close in the Chariot: but he that had changed himself into a Wolf, went into the wood again, and became a man.

Also in Livonia not many years since, continues our author, it fell out that the wife of a great Lord openly said that men could not be turned into Wolves. Whereupon one of the servants standing by declared that he would presently show her an example of that business, so he might do it with her permission. He goes alone into the cellar, and anon he comes out in the form of a wolf. The dogs ran after him through the fields to the wood, and they bit out one of his eyes though he defended himself stoutly enough. The next day he came with one eye to his Lady.

It is fresh in memory how the Duke of Prussia giving small credit to such a Witchcraft, compelled one who was cunning in this Sorcery, whom he held in chains to change himself into a Wolf; and he did so. Yet that he might not go unpunished for this Idolatry, he afterwards caused him to be burnt. For such heinous offences are severely punished both by Divine and Human Laws.

Caspar Peucer [16] says that although he long deemed the histories of werewolfery impossible and absurd, he was at last wholly convinced of their truth. In Livonia during the Christmas octave a boy who is lame in one foot goes round the countryside and summons in mysterious fashion all the warlocks, of whom there are very many. These varlets are compelled to follow the Devil's messenger, and if they delay another man soon visits them, armed with a huge whip knotted with iron, and they are eke compelled to hurry to the appointed station else he does not hesitate to flog them unmercifully tearing their flesh with his scourge. How bitter is the bondage of Satan! The wizards then all assemble at a certain rendezvous, and by their horrid art they change themselves into wolves. The man goes first with his huge whip, and the lupine train follow, evil folk who deceived by the Devil are persuaded that they are wolves. When they come to a river the leader strikes the water with his whip, and they seem to pass through by a dry path in horrid mockery of the miracle of the Red Sea, when Pharaoh's host were drowned. These wretches remain as wolves for a space of twelve days, during which they attack and devour cattle and sheep, but are not allowed to kill men. At the end of this period the glamour is dispersed and they return each to his home.

Simone Maiolo, Bishop of Volterra, in his *Dies Caniculares*,[17] has much to say of werewolfism and lycanthropy. He gathers instances and examples from many authorities when "*Rustici* illi ἀρκτολύκοι, quos nominamus *Bärwolff*, ambiguos lupos" come under discussion. He writes of a case of werewolfery which came under his notice not many years before, when a countryman was brought before a Duke of Muscovy, whose cattle he was said to have attacked and devoured in bestial form. This wretch was deformed and hideous to see, more like a beast than a man. His face and legs were covered with wounds, where he said he had been bitten by dogs when he was in the shape of a wolf. The Duke interrogated him straitly, and he confessed that twice a year, at Christmastide and about the Feast of S. John Baptist, Midsummer Day, there fell upon him a lupine ecstasy so that he rushed into the woods howling, and his shape was changed, hair covering his whole body. After the access he was weary to death and sick. In order to test the truth of the matter he was kept in hold for a year and more, but although the Lord's Birthday and S. John came round he was not metamorphosed. Clearly the man was a lycanthrope, not a werewolf.

Antonio de Torquemada, in his *Jardin de las Flores curiosas*,[18] jornada vi, tells of a Russian prince, who learning there was a shape-shifting warlock in his territory, ordered the varlet to be brought before him in chains, and then bade him give a sample of his skill. The man retired to a small room and presently came forth as a wolf, but the Prince let loose two fierce bandogs which he had in readiness, and these tore the wretched creature to pieces.

There are many werewolves in Russia, says Bishop Maiolo, haunting above all the Caucasus and Ural Mountains. The Yakuts of Siberia believe that every shaman is a past-master in shape-shifting, and moreover he keeps his soul or one of his souls incarnate in some animal mysteriously concealed where none may find it. The most powerful wizards are they whose souls are confined in elks, black bears, boars, fierce wolves, or eagles. The Samoyeds of the Turukhinsk say that every wizard leads a familiar about with him in the shape of a boar, guided by a magic belt. When the boar dies the shaman dies also, so closely knit is his soul to the familiar.[19] The Kamtchatkans fear the whale, the bear, and the wolf, whose names must never be mentioned when they are seen, for they understand human speech, they are warlocks in disguise.[20] The Siberians are loth to name the bear, who is termed of them "the little old man", "the master of the forest", "the sage", all phrases of utmost significance.[21]

Among the latest Soviet propaganda [22] is the utilization of fantastic legends about Lenin. In Siberia, among the aborigines, the story runs that Lenin was originally a bear, for the bear is the Siberian totem. "The bear Lenin lived for a long time in the virgin forest. There came a Russian general to the forest and tried to trap the bear. He placed a barrel of vodka in the forest, and Lenin having drunk it became intoxicated. Thus he fell into the hands of the Russian general who compelled him to wander about all over the world and to dance for him. Finally he escaped, became a man, and now he is revenging himself on all generals."

In Russia itself Lenin has been subtly introduced to the peasantry as a saint, and on the 1st May thousands of peasants light a candle in front of Lenin's picture just as they honour a real Saint upon his festa.

According to an article in *The Tablet*, 1st October, 1932, these abominations—amazing and incredible as it may seem— are even to be found in our midst, and we have "Anti-God Bolshevism on English soil". Thus the church at Sneyd, near Burslem, which is run on extremely ritualistic lines, is a centre of "The League of Militant Youth" which claims as its patrons "John Ball, the Communist leader of the English peasants, and Lenin, the Liberator"! A large red flag is suspended at the chancel arch, and Soviet emblems—the Sickle and the Hammer—are prominent. "In the vestry hangs a framed portrait of Lenin, before which, according to our Anglican informant, candles are sometimes lighted." [23] There is nothing new in all this. It is the heresy of the Cainites, so called from Cain, the first murderer, whom they praised and honoured most religiously, hailing him as their father.[24] The Cainites venerated and worshipped evil men, their father Cain; the rebels Core, Dathan, and Abiron, who went down alive into hell; the traitor Judas Iscariot. To-day they venerate Lenin. It is indeed nothing more nor less than Satanism, the worship of the Devil. It is of these that—as S. Epiphanius tells us—Our Lord said: "You are of your father the Devil, and the desires of your father you will do."[25] Origen, too, is justly scandalized that such heretics and worse than heretics should dare to claim that they are Christians.[26] So Satanism and socialism walk hand in hand, as was ever their wont, for Satan was the first socialist.

In an important study, "The Witches of the Gypsies," contributed by Dr. Heinrich von Wlislocki to the *Journal of the Gypsy Lore Society*,[27] in July, 1891, it is explained that these witches in order to preserve their health suck the blood of such men who are born at the waxing of the moon. The gypsies of Hungary and the Balkans term their victims *pañikotordimako* (literally *water-casks*). This belief prevails in Russia, Poland, and Hungary. The men who are thus vampirized fall into a kind of lycanthropy. They are characterized by a pale sunken countenance, hollow mournful eyes, swollen lips, and flabby inert arms. They are parched by a burning thirst, and soon can only utter bestial sounds, for the most part howling like wolves, and many at night are transformed into fierce wolves. Being larger and stronger than the natural wolf, these creatures become "wolf-kings", and their subjects must supply them with the finest meat. At dawn they recover the human shape, but they can eat nothing save raw flesh and they lap blood. In Romani they are termed *ruvanush* "wolf-man", from *ruv* "wolf" and *manush* "man".

Dr. Wlislocki further relates a story which was told him in reference to the murder of a Gypsy musician ten years before, that is to say in 1881. At Tórész, in the north of Hungary, there lived a Gypsy fiddler, named Kropan, who was very poor, and who in spite of his music could only get from the peasants a few coppers enough to buy a morsel of bread for himself and his wife. Remarking his wife's absences from home at night, he suspected an intrigue and watched her privily. When she deemed him asleep she slipped out of their hut, and in the dawn to his deadly fear the door opened and there slipped in a huge grey wolf carrying a mangled lamb in its mouth. The next thing he knew was that his wife was roasting him a dish of savoury meat. He said nothing, but from that day the woman provided him with the beast meats, sheep, calves, cows, and pigs. Kropan, indeed, used to sell quantities of meat in the nearest town, so that the villagers knew nothing of his transactions. He grew rich, and opened a fine inn where one could obtain dishes dirt cheap, so the whole neighbourhood flocked to him. The day arrived when suspicion was aroused, for the wolf had ravaged the countryside. The villagers bound Kropan and his wife, and the priest exorcized them, sprinkling them with holy water. As the drops touched her the woman shrieked as though she had been plunged into boiling oil, and this witch who nightly became a *ruvanush* disappeared. The peasants in a rage slew Kropan. The two ringleaders were imprisoned for six years in the jail at Ilova, but in 1881 they had been released and were living in Tórész.

It has been said, but quite incorrectly, that in Germany the werewolf was confined almost entirely to the Hartz Mountains. This region was indeed a centre of all known sorceries, but the depredations of the werewolf unhappily covered a far wider range.

Johannes Janssen, in his *History of the German People*,[28] part iii, chapter iii, is of opinion that the traditions of sorcery and shape-shifting which developed so grimly among the Germanic peoples to a large extent grew out of the old Teutonic system of supernatural beings, so that the gods and demi-gods came to be regarded as magicians, an idea embodied by Snorri Sturluson, who died in 1241, in the Ynglinga Saga. Like Wotan and Freyja, the warlock and sorcerers could change themselves into wolves and cats, the sacred animals of those deities. It was furthermore believed that such a metamorphosis was essential, at any rate the common folk either did not or could not distinguish correctly, and the most erroneous ideas began to prevail, inasmuch as Pope S. Gregory VII on 19th April, 1080, admonished King Harold of Denmark that he must no longer tolerate but root out the gruesome superstitions which filled people's lives with terror and dishonoured God by attributing almost unlimited power to the devils of darkness. This state of affairs was aggravated by the appearance of certain gnostic Manichaean sects who taught duality, that there were two conflicting, equally balanced principles, coexisting from eternity, the good and the bad.

An old German Penetential "Corrector",[29] 151, has: "Credidisti quod quidam credere solent, ut illae quae a uulgo parcae uocantur, ipsae, uel sint, uel possint hoc facere quod creduntur; id est dum aliquis homo nascitur, et tune ualeant ilium designare ad hoc quod uelint ut quandocunque ille homo uoluerit, in lupum transformari possit quod teutonica Werewulff uocatur, aut in aliam aliquam figuram? Si credidisti, quod unquam fieret aut esse possit, ut diuina imago in aliam formam aut in speciem transmutari possit ab aliquo, nisi ab omnipotente Deo, decem dies in pane et aqua debes poenitere."

Stephan Lanzkranna, Provost of S. Dorothy's in Vienna, did not hesitate in his *Himmelstrasse*, 1484, to class a heathen notion of werewolfery as a deception, more heathen than Christian, and a very great sin.

A Lübeck confession book, *Das Licht der Seele*, of the same year asks the penitent: "Have you done harm to anyone with the devilish art? Have you practised magic or witchcraft with the Holy Sacraments? Have you believed that people can become werewolves? . . . Let each one search his own conscience and make a clean breast to his Father Confessor."

In yet another confession book, widely circulated in the fifteenth century, the penitent is asked if he believes that "women can change themselves into cats, monkeys, and other animals, fly up through the air, and suck the blood of children?"

It was a false and pagan tradition that was thus denounced, but not the true and Christian belief in the reality of the forces of evil. The famous Augustinian preacher Gottschalk Hollen, who died in 1481, relates in his *Praeceptorium* how a woman who had been seemingly transformed by a witch into a mare was sprinkled with holy water and the glamour dispersed. Matthias von Kemnat, court chaplain to Frederick the Victorious of the Upper Palatinate, in his Chronicle of this Prince relates many similar instances of diabolical sorcery.[30]

During a Lenten course preached at Strassburg in 1508 by a famous pulpiteer, Dr. Johann Geiler von Kaisersberg, stirring discourses taken down by the Guardian of the Fransicans of the Strict Observance in that city, Father Johann Paul, who first published the collection in 1517 as *Die Emeis*,[31] is a sermon delivered on the third Sunday in Lent, with rubric, "Am dritten sontag den fasten, Occuli, predigt den doctor vor den Werwölffen." The good doctor discusses lycanthropy, apparently regarding werewolves as wolves of uncommon ferocity, who having tasted human flesh find it far more delicate than any other and desire it always. Hence they lie in wait to devour men. He certainly says that the Demon often appears in the shape of a wolf, and in his sermon on wild men of the woods he speaks of lycanthropes in Spain.

Guazzo in the *Compendium Maleficarum*,[32] book i, chapter 13, speaks of a shepherd named Petronius who was tried at Dalheim in 1581. "Whenever he felt moved with hatred or envy against the shepherds of neighbouring flocks (as is the way of such men) he used to change himself into a wolf by the use of certain incantations, and so for a long time escaped all suspicion as being the cause of the mutilation and death of his neighbours' sheep."

On 2nd September, 1663, at a meeting of the Royal Society, Sir Kenelm Digby "read a letter, sent to him out of the Palatinate, concerning some children snatched away in those parts by beasts, that had the appearance of wolves; but found killed after so strange a manner, that all people thereabout surmised, that they were not wolves, but *lycanthropi*, seeing, that nothing of the bodies of those children were devoured, but the heads, arms, and legs, severed from their-bodies, the skulls opened, and the brains taken out and scattered about the carcases, and the heart and bowels, in like manner, pulled out, but not devoured."[33]

18

One of the most famous of all German werewolf trials was that of Peter Stump (or Stumpf, Stube, Stubbe, Stub, as the name is indifferently spelled—and there are other variants), who was executed for his horrid crimes at Bedburg,[34] near Cologne, on 31st March, 1590. The case caused an immense sensation,[35] and was long remembered and quoted. Thus we have the following allusion by Samuel Rowlands in *The Knave of Harts*[36]:—

> A *German* (called *Peter Stumpe*) by charme,
> Of an inchanted Girdle, did much harme,
> Transform'd himselfe into a Wolfeish shape,
> And in a wood did many yeeres escape
> The hand of Iustice, till the Hang-man met him,
> And from a Wolfe, did with an halter set him:
> Thus counterfaiting shapes haue had ill lucke,
> Witnesse *Acteon* when he plaid the Bucke . . .

The contemporary pamphlet which gives an account of this werewolf is of the last rarity,[37] beyond which it has indeed such intrinsic interest that I have thought it well to reproduce it here in full.

A true Discourse.

Declaring the damnable life and death of one Stubbe Peeter, a most wicked Sorcerer, who in the likenes of a *Woolfe, committed many murders, continuing this* diuelish practise 25. yeeres, killing and de*uouring Men, Woomen, and* Children.

*Who for the same fact was ta*ken and executed the 31. of October *last past in the Towne of* Bedbur neer the Cittie of *Collin* in *Germany.*

Trulye translated out of the high Duch, according to the Copie printed in Collin, brought ouer into England by George Bores ordinary Poste, the xj. daye of this present Moneth of Iune 1590. who did both see and heare the same.

AT LONDON

Printed for Edward Venge, and are to be *solde in* Fleet-street *at the signe of the* Vine.

A most true Discourse, declaring the life and death of one Stubbe Peeter, being a most wicked Sorcerer.

Those whome the Lord dooth leaue to followe the Imagination of their own hartes, dispising his proffered grace, in the end through the hardnes of hart and contempt of his fatherly mercy, they enter the right path to perdicion and destruction of body and soule for euer: as in this present historie in perfect sorte may be seene, the strangenes whereof, together with the cruelties committed, and the long time therein continued, may driue many in doubt whether the same be truth or no, and the ratherfore that sundry falce & fabulous matters haue heertofore passed in print, which hath wrought much incredulitie in ye harts of all men generally, insomuch that now a daies fewe thinges doo escape be it neuer so certain, but that it is embased by the tearm of a lye or falce reporte. In the reading of this story, therfore I doo first request reformation of opinion, next patience to peruse it, because it is published for examples sake, and lastly to censure thereof as reason and wisdome dooth think conueniet, considering the subtilty that Sathan vseth to work the soules destruction, and the great matters which the accursed practise of Sorcery dooth effect, the fruites whereof is death and destruction for euer, and yet in all ages practised by the reprobate and wicked of the earth, some in one sort and some in another euen as the Deuill giueth promise to perfourme. But of all other that euer liued, none was comparable vnto this helhound, whose tiranny and cruelty did well declare he was of his Father the deuill, who was a murderer from the beginning, whose life and death and most bloody practises the discourse following dooth make just reporte. In the townes of Cperadt and Bedbur neer vnto Collin in high Germany, there was continually brought vp and nourished one Stubbe Peeter, who from his youth was greatly inclined to euill, and the practising of wicked Artes euen from twelue yeers of age till twentye, and so forwardes till his dying daye, insomuch that surfeiting in the Damnable desire of magick, negromancye, and sorcery, acquainting him selfe with many infernall spirites and feendes, insomuch that forgetting ye God that made him, and that Sauiour that shed his blood for mans redemption: In the end, careles of saluation gaue both soule and body to the deuil for euer, for small carnall pleasure in this life, that he might be famous and spoken of on earth, though he lost heauen thereby. The Deuill who hath a readye eare to listen to the lewde motions of cursed men, promised to give vnto him whatsoeuer his hart desired during his mortall life: wherupon this vilde wretch neither desired riches nor promotion, nor was his fancy satisfied with any externall or outward pleasure, but hauing a tirannous hart, and a most cruell bloody minde, he only requested that at his plesure he might woork his mallice on men, Women, and children, in the shape of some beast, wherby he might liue without dread or danger of life, and vnknowen to be the executor of any bloody enterprise, which he meant to commit: The Deuill who sawe him a fit instruemēt to perfourm mischeefe as a wicked feend pleased with the desire of wrong and destruction, gaue vnto him a girdle which being put about him, he was straight transfourmed into the likenes of a greedy deuouring Woolf, strong and mighty, with eyes great and large, which in the night sparkeled like vnto brandes of fire, a mouth great and wide, with most sharpe and cruell teeth, A huge body, and mightye pawes: And no sooner should he put off the same girdle, but presently he should appeere in his former shape, according to the proportion of a man, as if he had neuer beene changed.

21

Stubbe Peeter heerwith was exceedingly well pleased, and the shape fitted his fancye and agreeed best with his nature, being inclined to blood and crueltye, therfore satisfied with this strange and diuelish gifte, for that it was not troublesome nor great in cariage, but that it might be hidden in a small room, he proceeded to the execution of sundry most hainous and vilde murders, for if any person displeased him, he would incontinent thirst for reuenge, and no sooner should they or any of theirs walke abroad in the feeldes or about the Cittie, but in the shape of a Woolfe he would presentlye incounter them, and neuer rest till he had pluckt out their throates and teare their ioyntes a sunder: And after he had gotten a taste heerof, he tooke such pleasure and delight in shedding of blood, that he would night and day walke the Feelds, and work extreame cruelties. And sundry times he would goe through the Streetes of Collin, Bedbur, and Cperadt, in comely habit, and very ciuilly as one well knowen to all the inhabitants therabout, & oftentimes was he saluted of those whose freendes and children he had buchered, though nothing suspected for the same. In these places, I say, he would walke up and down, and if he could spye either Maide, Wife or childe, that his eyes liked or his hart lusted after, he would waite their issuing out of ye Cittie or town, if he could by any meanes get them alone, he would in the feeldes rauishe them, and after in his Wooluishe likenes cruelly murder them: yea often it came to passe that as he walked abroad in the feeldes, if he chaunste to spye a companye of maydens playing together, or else a milking of their Kine, in his Wooluishe shape he would incontinent runne among them, and while the rest escaped by flight, he would be sure to laye holde of one, and after his filthy lust fulfilled, he would murder her presentlye, beside, if he had liked or knowne any of them, look who he had a minde vnto, her he would pursue, whether she were before or behinde, and take her from the rest, for such was his swiftnes of foot while he continued a woolf: that he would outrunne the swiftest greyhound in that Countrye: and so muche he had practised this wickednes, that ye whole Prouince

22

was feared by the cruelty of this bloody and deuouring Woolfe. Thus continuing his diuelishe and damnable deedes within the compas of fewe yeeres, he had murdered thirteene yong Children, and two goodly yong women bigge with Child, tearing the Children out of their wombes, in most bloody and sauedge sorte, and after eate their hartes panting hotte and rawe, which he accounted dainty morsells & best agreeing to his Appetite.

Moreouer he vsed many times to kill Lambes and Kiddes and such like beastes, feeding on the same most vsually raw and bloody, as if he had beene a naturall Woolfe indeed, so that all men mistrusted nothing lesse then this his diuelish Sorcerie.

He had at that time liuing a faire yong Damosell to his Daughter, after whom he also lusted most vnnaturallye, and cruellye committed most wicked inceste with her, a most groce and vilde sinne, far surmounting Adultrye or Fornication, though the least of the three dooth driue the soule into hell fier, except hartye repentance, and the great mercy of God. This Daughter of his he begot when he was not altogither so wickedlye giuen, who was called by the name of Stubbe Beell, whose beautye and good grace was such as deserued commendacions of all those that knewe her: And such was his inordinate lust and filthye desire toward her, that he begat a Childe by her, dayly vsing her as his Concubine, but as an insaciate and filthy beast, giuen ouer to woork euil, with greedines he also lay by his owne Sister, frequenting her company long time euen according as the wickednes of his hart lead him: Moreouer being on a time sent for to a Gossip of his there to make merry and good cheere, ere he thence departed he so wunne the woman by his faire and flattering speech, and so much preuailed, yt ere he departed the house: he lay by her, and euer after had her companye at his commaund, this woman had to name Katherine Trompin, a woman of tall and comely stature of exceeding good fauour and one that was well esteemed among her neighbours. But his lewde and inordinat lust being not satisfied with the company of many Concubines, nor his wicked fancye contented with the beauty of any woman, at length the deuill sent vnto him a wicked spirit in the similitude and likenes of a woman, so faire of face and comelye of personage, that she resembled rather some heauenly Helfin then any mortall creature, so farre her beauty exceeded the choisest sorte of women, and with her as with his harts delight, he kept company the space of seuen yeeres, though in the end she proued and was found indeed no other then a she Deuil, notwithstanding, this lewd sinne of lecherye did not any thing asswage his cruell and bloody minde, but continuing an insatiable bloodsucker, so great was the ioye he took therin, that he accoūted no day spent in pleasure wherin he had not shed some blood not respecting so much who he did murder, as how to murder and destroy them, as the matter ensuing dooth manifest, which may stand for a speciall note of a cruell and hard hart. For hauing a proper youth to his sonne, begotten in the flower and strength of his age, the firste fruite of his bodye, in whome he took such ioye, that he did commonly call him his Hartes ease, yet so farre his delight in murder exceeded the ioye he took in his only Sonne, that thirsting after his blood, on a time he inticed him into the feeldes, and from thence into a Forrest hard by, where making excuse to stay about the necessaries of nature, while the yong man went on forward, incontinent in the shape and likenes of a Woolfe he encountred his owne Sonne, and there most cruelly slewe him, which doon, he presently eat the brains out of his head as a most sauerie and dainty delycious meane to staunch his greedye apetite: the most monstrous act that euer man heard off, for neuer was knowen a wretch from nature so far degenerate.

Long time he continued this vilde and villanous life, sometime in the likenes of a Woolfe, sometime in the habit of a man, sometime in the Townes and Citties, and sometimes in the Woods and thickettes to them adioyning, whereas the duche coppye maketh mention, he on a time mette with two men and one woman, whom he greatly desired to murder, and the better to bring his diuelish purpose to effect, doubting by them to be ouermatched and knowing one of them by name, he vsed this pollicie to bring them to their end. In subtill sorte he conuayed himselfe far before them in their way and craftely couched out of their sight, but as soone as they approched neere the place where he lay, he called one of them by his name, the partye hearing him selfe called once or twice by his name, supposing it was some familiar freend that in iesting sorte stood out of his sight, went from his companye towarde the place from whence the voice proceeded, of purpose to see who it was, but he was no sooner entred within the danger of this transformed man, but incontinent he was murdered in ye place, the rest of his company staying for him, expecting still his returne, but finding his stay ouer long: the other man lefte the woman, and went to looke him, by which means the second man was also murdered, the woman then seeing neither of both returne againe, in hart suspected that some euill had fan vpon them, and therfore with all the power she had, she sought to saue her selfe by flight, though it nothing preuailed, for good soule she was also soone ouertaken by this light footed Woolfe, whom when he had first deflowred, he after most cruelly murdered, the men were after found mangled in the wood, but the womans body was neuer after seene, for she the caitife had most rauenouslye deuoured, whose fleshe he esteemed both sweet and dainty in taste.

Thus this damnable Stubbe Peeter liued the tearme of fiue and twenty yeeres, unsuspected to be Author of so many cruell and vnnaturall murders, in which time he had destroyed and spoyled an vnknowen number of Men, Women, and Children, sheepe, Lambes, and Goates: and other Catttell, for when he could not through the warines of people drawe men, Women, or Children in his danger, then like a cruell and tirannous beast he would woorke his cruelty on brut beasts in most sauadge sort, and did act more mischeefe and cruelty then would be credible, although high Germany hath been forced to taste the trueth thereof.

By which meanes the inhabitantes of Collin, Bedbur and Cperadt, seeing themselues so greeuously endaungered, plagued, and molested by this greedy & cruel Woolfe, who wrought continuall harme and mischeefe, insomuch that few or none durst trauell to or from those places without good prouision of defence, and all for feare of this deuouring and fierce woolf, for oftentimes the Inhabitants found the Armes & legges of dead Men, Women, and Children, scattered vp and down the feelds to their great greefe and vexation of hart, knowing the same to be doone by that strange and cruell Woolfe, whome by no meanes they could take or ouercome, so that if any man or woman mist their Childe, they were out of hope euer to see it again aliue, mistrusting straight that the Woolfe had destroyed it.

And heere is to be noted a most strange thing which setteth foorth the great power and mercifull prouidence of God to ye comfort of eache Christian hart. There were not long agoe certain small Children playing in a Medowe together hard by ye town, where also some store of kine were feeding, many of them hauing yong calues sucking upon thē: and sodainly among these Children comes this vilde Woolfe running and caught a prittie fine Girle by the choller, with intent to pull out her throat, but such was ye will of God, that he could not pearce the choller of the Childes coate, being high and very well stiffened & close claspt about her neck, and therwithall the sodaine great crye of the rest of the childrē which escaped, so amazed the cattell feeding by, that being fearfull to be robbed of their young, they altogether came running against the Woolfe with such force that he was presently compelled to let goe his holde and to run away to escape ye danger of their hornes, by which meanes the Childe was preserued from death, and God be thanked remains liuing at this day.

And that this thing is true, Maister Tice Artine a Brewer dwelling at Puddlewharfe, in London, beeing a man of that Country borne, and one of good reputation and account, is able to iustifie, who is neere Kinsman to this Childe, and hath from thence twice receiued Letters conserning the same, and for that the firste Letter did rather driue him into wondering at the act then yeelding credit therunto, he had shortlye after at request of his writing another letter sent him, wherby he was more fully satisfied, and diuers other persons of great credit in London hath in like sorte receiued letters from their freends to the like effect.

Likewise in the townes of Germany aforesaid continuall praier was vsed vnto god that it would please him to deliuer thē from the danger of this greedy Woolfe.

And although they had practised all the meanes that men could deuise to take this rauenous beast, yet vntill the Lord had determined his fall, they could not in any wise preuaile: notwithstanding they daylye continued their purpose, and daylye sought to intrap him, and for that intent continually maintained great mastyes and Dogges of muche strength to hunt & chase the beast whersoeuer they could finde him. In the end it pleased God as they were in readines and prouided to meete with him, that they should espye him in his wooluishe likenes, at what time they beset him round about, and moste circumspectlye set their Dogges vpon him, in such sort that there was no means to escape, at which aduantage they neuer could get him before, but as the Lord deliuered Goliah into ye handes of Dauid, so was this Woolfe brought in danger of these men, who seeing as I saide before no way to escape the imminent danger, being hardly pursued at the heeles presently he slipt his girdle from about him, wherby the shape of a Woolfe cleane auoided, and he appeered presently in his true shape & likenes, hauing in his hand a staffe as one walking toward the Cittie, but the hunters whose eyes was stedfastly bent vpon the beast, and seeing him in the same place metamorphosed contrary to their expectation: it wrought a wonderfull amazement in their mindes, and had it not beene that they knewe the man so soone as they sawe him, they had surely taken the same to haue beene some Deuill in a mans likenes, but for as much as they knewe him to be an auncient dweller in the Towne, they came vnto him, and talking with him they brought him by communication home to his owne house, and finding him to be the man indeede, and no delusion

27

or phantasticall motion, they had him incontinent before the Maiestrates to be examined.

Thus being apprehended, he was shortly after put to the racke in the Towne of Bedbur, but fearing the torture, he volluntarilye confessed his whole life, and made knowen the villanies which he had committed for the space of xxv. yeeres, also he cōfessed how by Sorcery he procured of the Deuill a Girdle, which beeing put on, he forthwith became a Woolfe, which Girdle at his apprehension he confest he cast it off in a certain Vallye and there left it, which when the Maiestrates heard, they sent to the Vallye for it, but at their comming found nothing at al, for it may be supposed that it was gone to the deuil from whence it came, so that it was not to be found. For the Deuil hauing brought the wretch to al the shame he could, left him to indure the torments which his deedes deserued.

After he had some space beene imprisoned, the maiestrates found out through due examination of the matter, that his daughter Stubbe Beell and his Gossip Katherine Trompin, were both accessarye to diuers murders committed, who for the same as also for their leaud life otherwise committed, was arraigned, and with Stubbe Peeter condempned, and their seuerall Iudgementes pronounced the 28 of October 1589, in this manor, that is to saye: Stubbe Peeter as principall mallefactor, was iudged first to haue his body laide on a wheele, and with red hotte burning pincers in ten seueral places to haue the flesh puld off from the bones, after that, his legges and Armes to be broken with a woodden Axe or Hatchet, afterward to haue his head strook from his body, then to haue his carkasse burnde to Ashes.

Also his Daughter and his Gossip were Judged to be burned quicke to Ashes, the same time and day with the carkasse of the aforesaid Stubbe Peeter. And on the 31. of the same moneth, they suffered death accordingly in the town of Bedbur in the presence of many peeres & princes of Germany.

Thus Gentle Reader haue I set down the true discourse of this wicked man Stub Peeter, which I desire to be a warning to all Sorcerers and Witches, which vnlawfully followe their owne diuelish imagination to the vtter ruine and destruction of their soules eternally, from which wicked and damnable practice, I beseech God keepe all good men, and from the crueltye of their wicked hartes. Amen.

After the execution, there was by the aduice of the Maiestrates of the town of Bedbur a high pole set vp and stronglye framed, which first went through ye wheele wheron he was broken, whereunto also it was fastened, after that a little aboue the Wheele the likenes of a Woolfe was framed in wood, to shewe unto all men the shape wherein he executed those cruelties. Ouer that on the top of the stake the sorcerers head it selfe was set vp, and round about the Wheele there hung as it were sixteen peeces of wood about a yarde in length which represented the sixteene persons that was perfectly knowen to be murdered by him. And the same ordained to stand there for a continuall monument to all insuing ages, what murders by Stub Peeter was committed, with the order of his Iudgement, as this picture doth more plainelye expresse.

Witnesses that this is true.

Tyse Artyne.

William Brewar.

Adolf Staedt.

George Bores.

With diuers others that haue seen the same.

FOOTNOTES

[1] Konrad Maurer, *Die Bekerung des Norwegischen Stammes zum Christenthume*, 2 vols., Munich, 1856; vol. ii, p. 101 sqq. with the notes.

[2] In the Icelandic Poem of Hornklofi, beginning of the tenth century, a dialogue between a Valkyrie and a raven, the Valkyrie says: at berserkja reiðu vil bek ik spyrja, to which the raven

replies: Ulfhéðnar vóru, *they are called Wolfcoats.*

[3] See also Hertz, *Der Werwolf,* Stuttgart, 1861, p. 61 with the notes.

[4] Now generally considered to be derived from "bear-sark" (berr-serkr, *ursus* and shirt).

[5] Bear-men and bear-women are, of course, quite common in folk-lore and fable. Thus in Basile's *Pentamerone (Lo Cunto de li Cunti),* the Sixth Diversion of the Second Day, we have Antonella's tale of *The She-Bear: Le'Orza,* trattenemiento 6, jornata ii, ed. Napoli, 1788, tom. i, pp. 202–211; translated by Sir Richard Burton, 2 vols., London, 1893; vol. i, pp. 181–190. See also *The Pentamerone of Giambattista Basile* (Benedetto Croce), translated by N. M. Penzer, 2 vols., 1932; vol. i, pp. 170–7, "The She-Bear."

[6] *Furor athleticus,* of which a description is found in several Sagas, e.g. Snorri Sturluson's *Ynglinga Saga,* 6; *Hervaser Saga; Egils Saga,* 27; *Grettis Saga,* 42; *Eyrlyggia Saga,* 25; and others. For these see the collection, 3 vols., Rafn, Copenhagen, 1829–1830. See also the essay *De furore Bersercico* at the end of the *Kristni Saga,* in the edition *Biskupa Sögur,* vol. i, Copenhagen, 1858.

[7] See *Icelandic-English Dictionary,* Cleasby and Vigfusson, Oxford, 1874, under *ber-serkr,* p. 61.

[8] *Opera Omnia,* folio, Venetiis, 1591, p. 1009.

[9] Vol. ii, p. 108 sqq.

[10] *Volsunga saga; Det Norske old skriftselskabs samlinger viii:* ed. S. Bugge, 8vo, Christiana, 1865. *Volsunga Saga,* translated from the Icelandic by Eiríkr Magnússon and William Morris, ed. by H. H. Sparling, London, 1888, chapters viii and (for King Siggeir's mother) v.

[11] *Svenska Folk-Visor . . . af* Er. Gust. Geijer och Arv. Aug. Afzelius, 3 vols., Stockholm, 1814–16. Tredje delen (1816), pp. 119–120. The line annotated runs: "Och som'a skapte hon till *ulfvar* grä."

[12] Albert Krantz of Hamburg, died in December, 1517. *Chronica,* folio, 1546, pp. 35–6.

[13] Typis Monasterii S. Galli. Folio, 1690, "Nunc primum . . . publicae luci datum," pp. 112 and 120.

[14] *Speculum Maius: Speculum Historiale*, tom. iv, p. 342, verso; ed. folio, Venetiis, 1591.

[15] There is an English version and abridgement, *A Compendious History of the Goths, Swedes, & Vandals*, folio, 1658. In this the reference is Book xviii, chapters 32 and 33. I have adopted a phrase here and there from this old version, but it must be used cautiously as there are many important omissions.

[16] *Commentarius de Prœcipuis Generibus Diuinationum*, Witebergae, 1572, pp. 130-4.

[17] Folio, Offenbaci ad Moenum, 1691: Colloquium ii, pp. 28-9; Coll. iii, pp. 432-6. The good Bishop does not neglect the *"Sagae in feles conuersae"*. He also mentions the water-ordeal. Indeed, the whole Colloquium iii, *De Sagis*, should be read. It should perhaps be mentioned that some ascribe this section to George Draud of Davernheim (1573-1635).

[18] Salamanca, 1570. This book ran into several French editions as the *Hexameron*, "Fait en Hespagnol et mis en françois par Gabriel Chappuys, Tourangeau," Lyons, 16mo, 1579.

[19] *Journal of the Anthropological Institute*, vol. xxiv, 1895, pp. 133-4; Professor V. M. Mikhailoviskij, "Shamanism in Siberia and European Russia."

[20] G. W. Steller, *Beschreibung von dem Lande Kamtschatka*, Frankfort and Leipzig, 1774, p. 276.

[21] P. Labbé, *Un Bagne russe, l'île de Sakhaline*, Paris, 1903, p. 231. Cf. the name given to a bear in the *Pentamerone*, tratteniemento vi, jornata ii, *Le'Orza*, ed. Napoli, 1788, tom. i, pp. 202–211, "Ma lo Prencepe decenno all'Orza, Chiappino mio, non me vuoje cocenare?" (p. 210). "But the Prince said to the Bear, Teddy dear, won't you cook me something?" Porta has a comedy *La Chiappinaria*.

[22] *Anglo-Russian News*, No. 188, 18th January, 1929. "Legends of Lenin as Propaganda."

[23] Apparently in the vestry of All Saints, Manchester, is enshrined the portrait of a dramatist, George Bernard Shaw. Can folly go further? I do not know whether tapers are lighted before this

new Beato or Saint or whatever he is esteemed to be. See *The Tablet*, vol. 160, No. 4821, pp. 425–6, "Comprehensive Indeed!" Also, *Tablet*, 8th Oct., pp. 457–8; 15th Oct., p. 495; 22nd Oct., pp. 525–6; 29th Oct., p. 559; 5th Nov., p. 592.

[24] "ἃ πὸ το Κάϊν εἰληφότες . . . Οὗτοι γὰρ τὸν Κάϊν ἐπανοσι, καί πατέρα εἰαυτῶν τοον τάττουσι." And a little later: "'Επαινοσι γὰρ τὸν Κάϊν καί τὸν 'Ιονδαυ." S. Epiphanius Aduersus Haereses, lib. i, tom. iii. Migne, *Patr. Gr.*, vol. xli, 653–666. See also S. Irenaeus, *Contra Haereses*, lib. i, cap. xxxi. Migne, *P.G.*, vol. vii, 704–6, "De Caianis."

[25] S. John's Gospel, viii, 44.

[26] *Contra Celsum*, vi, 28. Origen is speaking directly of the Ophites who were Satanists even as the Cainites. "τοσοτον ἀποδέονσι τοείαι Χριστιανοί, ὥστε οὐκ λαττον Κέλσου κατηγυρεν αὐτονς τοΙησο"

[27] Vol. iii, No. 1, pp. 38–45.

[28] *Geschichte des deutschen Volkes seit dem Aufgang der Mittelalter*, 6 vols., Freiburg, 1878–9; new ed. Ergänzt und herausg. von Ludwig Pastor, 8 vols., Freiburg, 1897. Eng. tr. *History of the German People after the Close of the Middle Ages*, 16 vols., by M. A. Mitchell and A. M. Christie. Vol. xvi (1910), tr. A. M. Christie, pp. 216–526.

[29] Hermann Joseph Schmitz, *Die Bussbücher und die Bussdisciplin der Kirche*, Band ii. Düsseldorf, 1892, p. 442.

[30] For these details the authority is Dr. Heinrich Geffeken, who is quoted by Janssen, Eng. tr., vol. xvi, pp. 230–2 and notes.

[31] "Die Emeis. Dis ist das büch von der Omeissen, und dauch Herr der Künnig ich diente gern. Und sacht von Eichtenschafft der Omeissen. Und gibt underweisung von den Unholden oder Hexen, und von gespenst der geist, und von dem Wütenden heer wunderbarlich." Folio, 1517. (Bodley, fol. Θ. 583.) p. xxxxi. See also the Sermon "Von wilden Mannen," p. xxxxi (recto). Johann Geiler was born in 1445 at Schaffhausen and lived at Strassburg in 1508. For further details see Joseph Hansen, *Quellen und Untersuchungen zur Geschichte des Hexenwahns*, Bonn, 1901,

pp. 284–291.

[32] Eng. tr., 1929, p. 52.

[33] Thomas Bird, *History of the Royal Society of London*, 4 vols., 1756–7, vol. i, p. 300.

[34] Bedburg to-day is a little town of 2,925 inhabitants. It is situated on the Erit, an affluent of the left of the Rhine. The railway station (the second after Düsen) is on the Aix-la-Chapelle to Neuss line.

[35] There is a reference by Delrio, *Disquisitionum Magicarum*, liber ii, q. xviii, ed. Moguntiae, 1603, pp. 165–6, who mentions the sensation caused by the trial. Verstegan (Rowlands), *Restitution of Decayed Intelligence*, 1605, p. 237, mentions that "One *Peeter Stump* for beeing a were-wolf, and hauing killed thirteen children, two women, and one man was at *Bedbur* not far from *Cullen* in the yeare 1589 put vnto a very terrible death". See also Edward Fairfax, *Daemonologia*, ed. Grainge, 1882, p. 97.

[36] *The Knave of Harts. Haile Fellow well met.* 4to, 1612. *Epigram* preceeding Epilogue, p. 47.

[37] The only two copies of which I have any knowledge, and I believe none others have been traced, are those in the British Museum and in the Lambeth Library respectively. The original is black letter. I have corrected one misprint; p. 258, l. 45, where I read "no delusion" for "no selusion".